EARLY BIRD
STORIES

Little Fish
and Big Fish

Early ★ Reader

First American edition published in 2019 by Lerner Publishing Group, Inc.

An original concept by Lou Treleaven
Copyright © 2019 Lou Treleaven

Illustrated by Dean Gray

First published by Maverick Arts Publishing Limited

Maverick
arts publishing

Licensed Edition
Little Fish and Big Fish

Lerner Publications Company
A division of Lerner Publishing Group, Inc.
241 First Avenue North
Minneapolis, MN 55401 USA

For reading levels and more information, look up this title at www.lernerbooks.com.

Main body text set in Mikado a. Typeface provided by HVD Fonts.

Library of Congress Cataloging-in-Publication Data

Names: Treleaven, Lou, author. | Gray, Dean, illustrator.
Title: Little Fish and Big Fish / by Lou Treleaven ; illustrated by Dean Gray.
Description: First American edition. | Minneapolis : Lerner Publications, 2019. |
    Series: Early bird readers. Yellow (Early bird stories).
Identifiers: LCCN 2018017849 (print) | LCCN 2018033692 (ebook) |
    ISBN 9781541543355 (eb pdf) | ISBN 9781541541696 (lb : alk. paper) |
    ISBN 9781541546325 (pb : alk. paper)
Subjects: LCSH: Readers—Fishes. | Readers (Primary) | Fishes—Juvenile
    literature.
Classification: LCC PE1119 (ebook) | LCC PE1119 .T757 2019 (print) |
    DDC 428.6/2—dc23

LC record available at https://lccn.loc.gov/2018017849

Manufactured in the United States of America
1-45343-38993-6/27/2018

EARLY BIRD STORIES

Little Fish and Big Fish

Lou Treleaven

Illustrated by
Dean Gray

Lerner Publications ◆ Minneapolis

Little Fish and Big Fish

go for a swim.

Little Fish is little.

Big Fish is big.

"I am the **biggest** fish in the sea," says Big Fish.

A rock moves.

It is not a rock. It is a fish.

"I am the **biggest** fish in the sea,"

says the very **big** fish.

A boat moves.

It is not a boat. It is a fish.

"I am the **biggest** fish in the sea," says the very **very big** fish.

They swim to a cave.

It is not a cave. It is a fish.

"I am the **biggest** fish in the sea," says the very very **very big** fish.

"And you will all be my supper!"

"Not me," says Little Fish.

Little Fish gets in a shell.

"Ow!" says a little crab.

"You sat on me, you big, big fish!"

Quiz

1. What do Little Fish and
   Big Fish do?
   a) Have supper
   b) Go for a swim
   c) Go to sleep

2. It is not a rock. It is . . . ?
   a) A crab
   b) A shell
   c) A fish

3. Where do the fish swim to?
   a) A boat
   b) A rock
   c) A cave

4. What does the very very very big
   fish want to do?
   a) Have the fish for his supper.
   b) Sit on the fish.
   c) Give the fish a hug.

5. What does the crab think
   Little Fish is?
   a) Kind
   b) Big
   c) Bad

EARLY BIRD STORIES™

Leveled for Guided Reading

Early Bird Stories have been edited and leveled by leading educational consultants to correspond with guided reading levels. The levels are assigned by taking into account the content, language style, layout, and phonics used in each book.

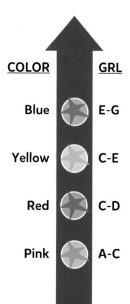

COLOR	GRL
Blue	E-G
Yellow	C-E
Red	C-D
Pink	A-C